KING of MAGIC, MAN of GLASS

A GERMAN FOLK TALE

RETOLD BY Judith Kinter

ILLUSTRATED BY Dirk Zimmer

CLARION BOOKS/New York

Clarion Books
a Houghton Mifflin Company imprint
215 Park Avenue South, New York, NY 10003
Text copyright © 1998 by Judith Kinter
Illustrations copyright © 1998 by Dirk Zimmer

Printed in the USA.

Library of Congress Cataloging-in-Publication Data
Kinter, Judith.
King of magic, man of glass : a German folk tale / retold by Judith Kinter ;
illustrated by Dirk Zimmer.
p.   cm.
Summary: Even after his magical godfather sends him home from the
Black Forest with a sackful of coins, a young man refuses to listen to
his mother and be content with his simple life.
ISBN 0-395-79730-6
[1. Fairy tales. 2. Folklore—Germany.] I. Zimmer, Dirk, ill. II. Title.
PZ8.1.K616G1   1998
398.2'0943'021—dc21   97-25044
CIP
AC

HOR 10 9 8 7 6 5 4 3 2 1

To my grandmother, who passed the story on to me,
so I can pass it on to you.
—J.K.

For Anja.
—D.Z.

In those long-ago days of magical godfathers in the Black Forest of Germany, there lived a poor, hard-working widow named Anna and her son, Rudolf, who was always complaining.

"Daylight already!" Rudolf grumbled every morning when the sun opened his eyes and he rolled out of his straw bed.

"What miserable rags!" he muttered, yanking on the shirt his mother had neatly patched.

"Oh, my poor back!" he groaned as he staggered to the village market with a heavy sack of charcoal on his back.

Rudolf never glanced at the carpet of bluebells rippling over the meadow in the fresh spring breeze. He never smiled at his mother's cheerful humming as she swept the dirt floor of the hut. And at night, while he tended the kiln that blackened wood scraps into charcoal, he never gazed up at the dazzling blanket of stars.

"Our life is good, my son," Anna said as they sat by the warm kiln, eating their evening meal of turnips. "We have lived to see yet another beautiful day."

"How can you call this living?" asked Rudolf, flinging his turnip rinds to Max, their dog. "What's good about peddling charcoal all day and tending a smoky kiln half the night? And for what? Turnips! Our life is no good!"

"My son," said Anna with a sigh, "I have raised you the best way I know how, and so it pains me to see you so unhappy. But perhaps there is one way to help you find happiness. Now listen well." She peered into the Black Forest and lowered her voice to a whisper. "You are the son of a seventh son, and because of that you have a very special godfather. A godfather who has magical powers!"

"Why didn't you tell me this before?" Rudolf cried out. "How can I find him?"

"It is not so simple," Anna responded. "Your god-father can help only a godchild with a heart as pure as glass, someone who is kind to people and animals alike."

"Well, I have never hurt anyone," Rudolf answered. "Don't I feed Max my turnip rinds every night? Mother, you must tell me how to find my godfather!"

Gazing at Rudolf with tenderness and concern, Anna explained, "He is the King of Magic and is called 'Glass Man.' He lives in the tallest pine tree on the highest mountain in the Black Forest. The pine tree is encircled by seven fir trees. To enter this magic circle, you must first walk three times around the seven fir trees, touching each one with the palm of your hand without making a sound. Then, as you enter the circle, you lay a gift at the foot of the tall pine and say clearly:

> *King of Magic,*
> *Man of Glass,*
> *Please show yourself to me.*

And if he so chooses, your godfather will appear. But I must warn you, my son, that his magic is very powerful. Please be careful."

The very next morning, Rudolf heaved a huge sack of charcoal onto his back, and with Max following closely behind, he set out for the top of the highest mountain. It was a long, hard journey, and Rudolf wished he had brought a lighter gift.

At long last he reached the circle of seven trees. It was so quiet, Rudolf feared that even his breathing might break the stillness. Max whimpered at his heels.

Stepping as softly as he could, Rudolf walked around the circle, touching each fir tree with the palm of his hand. Then he entered the circle, laid the sack of charcoal at the foot of the tall pine, closed his eyes, and called:

> *King of Magic,*
> *Man of Glass,*
> *Please show yourself to me.*

Suddenly there was a strange rustling in the tree branches, followed by a high laugh that sounded like tinkling glass. Rudolf opened his eyes.

The circle of trees glistened like the sunshine. The pine needles on the ground shimmered a frosty white. Everything had turned to glass.

Again came the tinkling sound. Gray smoke enveloped the tall pine, and a pair of tiny black boots suddenly appeared, swinging from one of its branches.

Startled, Rudolf stumbled backward. As soon as he stepped outside the circle of pines, the boots faded from sight. Rudolf took a trembling step forward. The boots reappeared, and a voice cut the crisp air like splintering icicles. "Make up your mind. Do you want to see your godfather or not?"

As Rudolf stood there open-mouthed, a long, gold pipe appeared in midair, followed by baggy red pants, a wide gold belt, a bright green coat with silver trim, and finally a red face; with a white beard and piercing blue eyes that stared from under a tall black hat. The man was made of sparkling, clear glass and was no bigger than a turnip.

What sort of godfather is this? Rudolf thought.

"Speak up, Rudolf!" the little Glass Man said.

"Please, Godfather, sir," Rudolf stammered, unsure how to address such a strange creature. "I came here to ask for your help. I can no longer bear my life. All I do is gather wood, tend the kiln, sell my charcoal at the market . . . and all I get for my trouble is *turnips!*"

The Glass Man laughed and clicked his heels. "Ah, but your life is good, Rudolf. You work hard. You eat simple food, but you have enough. You have a home and a mother who loves you. What more do you need?"

"But Godfather," Rudolf protested, "my life is terrible! Winter storms spit snow in my eyes as I labor under my charcoal sack in winter, and winds blow through the cracks of our cottage as I shiver in my straw bed at night. In the summer the sun burns the soles of my feet on the cobblestones. The son of a seventh son deserves better!"

The Glass Man's eyes darkened and his voice cracked. "Imbecile! Take your charcoal sack and be gone!" And right before Rudolf's eyes, the little Glass Man slowly faded in a cloud of smoke. The trees turned green again and the brown pine needles crackled softly underfoot. Max sidled up to Rudolf, whining.

"Some godfather!" Rudolf mumbled. "I went to all this trouble for nothing!"

Furious, he yanked the sack over his shoulder and trudged back down the mountain. The longer he walked, the heavier the sack felt. He would have tossed it aside, but he knew how hard he would have to work to fill another.

When he stomped through the door of the cottage, his mother had supper warming for him on the kiln.

"What a rotten turnip, that godfather!" Rudolf cried, slamming his sack on the ground. With a clink the sack split open, and coins gushed out in a silver stream.

Anna gasped.

"We're rich!" Rudolf shouted, scooping up coins and tossing them in the air. "No more turnips for us!" he cried. "Only the finest bread and cheese . . . and only the best red wine!"

"Don't be so hasty, my son," Anna warned as she carefully gathered up the coins. "We should buy ourselves a cow with this money."

"As you please, Mother," Rudolf replied, and he divided the coins into two piles.

With her share Anna bought a milk cow. Rudolf, however, spent his coins feasting on fine bread, cheese, and wine. But in the evenings, when he heard merry laughter and music coming from the village, he wished he had enough money to buy some fine clothes, so that he could dance on the village green with the other young people.

"I'm going back to my godfather to ask him for more money," Rudolf told his mother.

"Rudolf, you should be happy with what you have!" Anna cried.

But the very next morning, Rudolf set off up the mountain with Max bounding after him. This time he took a larger sack of charcoal, thinking it would hold more coins. The sack was twice as heavy, and the way to the tall pine tree at the top of the highest hill seemed twice as long.

With his palms open, Rudolf once again touched each of the seven fir trees, then laid down his gift at the foot of the pine.

He closed his eyes, and called:

King of Magic,
Man of Glass,
Please show yourself to me.

When he opened his eyes, he saw that again the forest had turned into shimmering glass.

"Back again, my son?" came the Glass Man's icy voice. "What could you possibly want now?"

"Godfather," Rudolf said, "the son of a seventh son deserves a little fun. If I had a fine suit, I could dance on the village green with the maiden of my choice."

This time the Glass Man did not laugh; he simply faded away except for his blue eyes that pierced the darkening sky.

"Ungrateful godson," snapped the Glass Man's voice. "My gift has not helped you one bit. Take your sack and leave! And don't ever come back! Never!" The eyes vanished, and the glass forest turned green again.

Filled with anger, Rudolf dragged the heavy sack home.

And once again he found his sack full of coins.

"Life is good, Rudolf!" his mother cried. "Now we can buy a little farm, with a goat-bell jingling on a red gate and a flock of white sheep, and be content for the rest of our lives!"

"Do whatever you wish, Mother," Rudolf answered, counting out his share. "I shall dance on the village green!"

And he did. In his elegant new boots and a handsome new suit of clothes, Rudolf danced the summer away. Every girl glanced his way now. But they glanced in vain.

"I would never settle down with a girl from this dull place," Rudolf told his mother. "The son of a seventh son deserves the best. I'm going to see my godfather and tell him this time he must do something special for me!"

"No, Rudolf!" Anna cried. "Not three times!"

"Don't worry, Mother. I'm not afraid of my godfather."

Rudolf kicked Max aside and strode up the mountain that very afternoon, complaining the whole time of the steepness of the path and the scratches the bushes made on his shiny new boots.

Impatiently he slapped the fir trees, forgetting he had no gift, and boldly shouted:

King of Magic,
Man of Glass,
Please show yourself to me.

A heavy hush fell over the circle. Then a voice split the silence like a sharp sword. "How dare you come again!"

The ground trembled. The tall pine tree shook, and the Glass Man appeared. But it was not a smiling little Glass Man, clicking his heels.

Towering higher than the tallest tree, his eyes flashing blue lightning, and wearing a fiery red robe and a golden crown—he was majestic.

"Only the curse of what you ask for can save you now!" he thundered as he spiraled up in billowing black clouds and vanished in flashes of fire. The earth roared and shook.

Rudolf fled down the mountain. Icy gales pushed him into trees. Hail pelted his back. Torrents of rain blinded his eyes and choked his breath.

When he finally stumbled into the cottage, his fine clothes ripped to shreds, he looked like a drenched, ragged street urchin. His shaking fingers could barely bolt the door.

"Thank goodness you're alive," his mother gasped, hugging him.

As he was taking off his soggy jacket, Rudolf felt something heavy in his pocket. "What is this useless thing?" he asked, puzzled.

It was shaped like a pine cone but was made of sparkling, clear glass. With a faint tinkling sound, the cone cracked open and filled Rudolf's hands with gold coins. In surprise, Rudolf dropped the coins. His hands filled up again. No matter how many times he emptied the glass cone, his hands filled with coins.

"My godfather was joking!" Rudolf cried with joy. "This is not a curse! At last he has given me enough money to live as the son of a seventh son deserves. We shall live like kings!"

Anna shrank back. "No, no," she said, her voice trembling.

"Say no more, Mother," Rudolf answered, putting the cone back in his pocket. "I'm off to see the world."

First he bought a castle high above the river Rhine. It had seven gold towers, and white swans glided over the waters surrounding it. But soon Rudolf grew bored. "What a chilly, dark cavern this castle is," he complained. "My old, drafty hut was cozier than this. I will go to sunny Rome."

In Rome Rudolf visited elegant cathedrals with glis-
tening domes and bells that sang like angels. But soon
he was bored again. "The domes are tarnished, and
the bells clang like hollow tin. The sunrise over my
hilltop was more glorious, and the goat-bell on our
gate jingled more sweetly. I will go to beautiful
Paris."

Rudolf sipped wine in the finest cafes and walked among the bright flowers along the Seine. But soon he was bored there, too. "Hmmph! Such garish flowers. The bluebells in my meadow are prettier than these."

And so Rudolf moved from country to country. But with each new place he visited, his disappointment grew and his heart felt heavier.

39

Finally he could think of nowhere else to go. Throwing away a half-eaten chocolate, he cried, "Sawdust! My old turnips were more tasty! Is there nothing wonderful anywhere? My heart is heavy and hard as . . ." He put his hand over his heart. It felt hard, with only a faint beat. ". . . as glass!" cried Rudolf, shaking out his pockets and throwing all the gold coins onto the ground.

Children scampered after the coins as they rolled down the street.

"Take them!" Rudolf shouted. "They are of no use to me! I am cursed!" He was about to hurl the glass cone after the coins when he heard the faintest tinkling sound from inside it, and in a flash of light the little Glass Man appeared inside the cone.

"Oh, Godfather," Rudolf whispered. "How right you were. My greed has made my heart as hard as glass."

The Glass Man nodded his head and smiled; then he was gone. At that very instant Rudolf felt his heart begin to beat more strongly.

He looked into the cone once more and saw his mother, standing by the red gate, looking down the mountain with tears in her eyes.

"What have I done!" Rudolf cried. "I worked hard, but it was honest work. My food was simple, but there was always enough. I had a home and a mother who loved me. The little Glass Man was right. I already had all I needed."

So Rudolf returned home with an armful of bluebells for his mother.

He set the glass pine cone over the kiln and he
never touched it again.

AUTHOR'S NOTE

While people often associate German tales with the brothers Grimm, the origins of *King of Magic, Man of Glass* can be traced to Willhelm Hauff, a young German tutor from Stuttgart. Hauff rose to enormous fame in the early nineteenth century by publishing a collection of popular fairytales, among them *The Stone Cold Heart.* Over the years, many tellings and translations have altered this tale while retaining its basic and enduring themes of family relationships and moral judgment. Today, this story is a window on a world long since past, but it continues to entertain us with its winsome characters and thoughtful message.